Hello, Family Members,

Learning to read is one of the most important accomplishments of early childhood. **Hello Reader!** books are designed to help children become skilled readers who like to read. Beginning readers learn to read by remembering frequently used words like "the," "is," and "and"; by using phonics skills to decode new words; and by interpreting picture and text clues. These books provide both the stories children enjoy and the structure they need to read fluently and independently. Here are suggestions for helping your child *before*, *during*, and *after* reading:

Before

- Look at the cover and pictures and have your child predict what the story is about.
- Read the story to your child.
- Encourage your child to chime in with familiar words and phrases.
- Echo read with your child by reading a line first and having your child read it after you do.

During

- Have your child think about a word he or she does not recognize right away. Provide hints such as "Let's see if we know the sounds" and "Have we read other words like this one?"
- Encourage your child to use phonics skills to sound out new words.
- Provide the word for your child when more assistance is needed so that he or she does not struggle and the experience of reading with you is a positive one.
- Encourage your child to have fun by reading with a lot of expression . . . like an actor!

After

- Have your child keep lists of interesting and favorite words.
- Encourage your child to read the books over and over again. Have him or her read to brothers, sisters, grandparents, and even teddy bears. Repeated readings develop confidence in young readers.
- Talk about the stories. Ask and answer questions. Share ideas about the funniest and most interesting characters and events in the stories.

I do hope that you and your child enjoy this book.

—Francie Alexander
Chief Education Officer
Scholastic Education

D0645366

To Lia
—G.M.

To Isaac, Wes, Leo, and Arlo
—B.L.

The author gratefully acknowledges Jordan Riesman for his contribution to this book.

No part of this publication may be reproduced, or stored in a retrieval system, or transmitted in any form or by any means, electronic, mechanical, photocopying, recording, or otherwise, without written permission of the publisher. For information regarding permission, write to Scholastic Inc., Attention: Permissions Department, 557 Broadway, New York, NY 10012.

Text copyright © 2003 by Grace Maccarone.
Illustrations copyright © 2003 by Betsy Lewin.
All rights reserved. Published by Scholastic Inc.
SCHOLASTIC, HELLO READER, CARTWHEEL BOOKS, and associated logos
are trademarks and/or registered trademarks of Scholastic Inc.

Library of Congress Cataloging-in-Publication Data

Maccarone, Grace.
The sleep over / by Grace Maccarone ; illustrated by Betsy Lewin.
p. cm. — (Hello reader! Level 1)
Summary: Sam has a wonderful time at his friend Dan's house playing games, eating dinner, and watching a movie, but when it's time to go to sleep, not even Huggy Bear can help.
ISBN: 0-439-38575-X
[1. Sleep overs — Fiction. 2. Stories in rhyme.] I. Lewin, Betsy, ill. II. Title. III. Series.
PZ8.3.M127 S1 2003
[E]—dc21

2002002733

10 9 8 7 6 5 4 3 03 04 05 06 07
24

Printed in the U.S.A.
First printing, February 2003

First-Grade Friends

The Sleep Over

by Grace Maccarone
Illustrated by Betsy Lewin

Hello Reader! — Level 1

SCHOLASTIC INC.
Cartwheel BOOKS®
New York Toronto London Auckland Sydney
Mexico City New Delhi Hong Kong Buenos Aires

Sam packs PJ's,
underwear.
Sam does not pack
Huggy Bear.

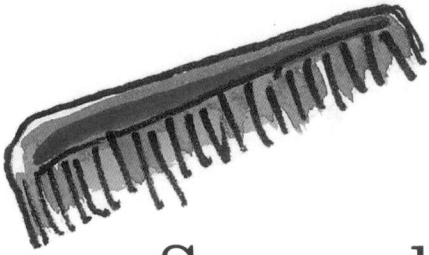

Sam packs a comb,
fresh clothes to wear,
a toothbrush . . .

and his Huggy Bear.

Sam gets inside
the SUV.

"Tonight I'll sleep at Dan's.
Yippee!"

"Come here," says Mom.
"Let me kiss you.
Have fun tonight.
I will miss you!"

"Come in," Dan says.
"I'm glad you came.
Max is here.
Let's play a game."

They play a game,
then play another.

"It's time to eat, boys,"
calls Dan's mother.

Sam is hungry,
so Sam eats a
salad and a slice
of pizza.

They brush their teeth

and wash their faces,

put on pajamas . . .

and pick their places.

"Let's watch a movie on TV,"
Dan says.
The other boys agree.

At ten o'clock,
the movie ends.
It's sleepy time
for three good friends.

Dan's mom comes in
to close the light.
She says, "Good night.
Sweet dreams. Sleep tight."

But Sam needs Huggy.

He goes to get her.

Now Sam has Huggy,
and Sam feels better.

But Sam can't sleep.
He misses his mother.
He misses his dad.
He misses his brother.

He tells Dan's mom.

She tells Sam's dad.

Now Dad is here,
and Sam is glad.

So Sam goes home.

He gets there fast.

And Sam is in
his bed —
at last!

When morning comes,
Sam's on his way
to Dan's where he'll
eat eggs and play.

The three boys
have a happy day!